UGLYDOLLS

Written by Emily Skwish

we make books come alive®

pi kids Phoenix International Publications, Inc.

Chicago • London • New York • Hamburg • Mexico City • Paris • Sydney

It's a beautiful day in Uglyville! Of course, for Moxy, every day is beautiful—that is to say, special, one-of-a-kind, and adorably quirky. Anything could happen, and today could be the day!

These Uglyville citizens are ready to get their sweat on. Can you find them as they shape up and work out?

Not everything happens in the center of town. Ice-Bat chills out in the temperature-controlled comfort of her ice cave (which also happens to be the mini-fridge in the back of her friend Wage's diner).

When friends come to visit Ice–Bat, they all scream for ice cream. Can you find these friends holding cold confections?

Lots of Uglyville's citizens are nautical by nature. When the boat race begins, it's all dolls on deck. Shiver me stuffins, mateys!

Gotta regatta? Search the seas for these cuddly commodores:

Life is a dream in Uglyville! But wait, this looks like an actual dream: there's flying, aliens, and weird little red dolls everywhere...um, doesn't everybody have this dream?

Fly around with Dream-Bat and find these outer space friends:

Good morning, Uglyville! Last night's wild dreams were so much fun, some residents have put on costumes this morning to keep it surreal. Others put on costumes because the panda suit was the only thing that was clean.

Take a look around the town and find these dressed-up denizens:

A button saved is a button earned. Uglyville's primary unit of currency can be used to hold up pants. Now that's valuable! The Uglyville bank also has a special window for folks who prefer to get paid in cookies.

BANK ON iT.

BUX in a BOX

$

FOUNDER

BUX in a BOX

ALMOST FREE COFFEE

Scan the bank lobby for these cookie-lovers:

Special delivery! The back room of the post office is where Uglyville's letters and packages are prepared to go out into the world. Their super high-tech equipment and organization systems ensure that nothing ever gets lost!

Air mail! Find the UglyDolls who just found these letters:

Babo's Cookies is the place to go if you want your cookies ridiculous-sized! And today Babo is facing a ridiculous-sized crowd, as everyone in Uglyville comes looking for freshly baked treats.

MiLK

FLOUR

MAKE BAKE TAKE

Cookies

Jumbo

BIG

Ridiculous

cream cheese

A few customers have brought their own snacks to munch on while they wait. Look for these *un*baked goods that have snuck into the bakery:

It's a sign! Head back to Uglyville's workout and find these posters and signs around downtown:

The weather inside the ice cave is delightful...if you have your winter gear! Ski back and find these cozy characters in scarves and hats:

Don't forget the sunscreen—or your sunglasses! Sail back to the boat race and find these citizens wearing slick shades:

Wake up and search the dream scene! Find all these funny little red guys while you're at it:

It's a great day to pup it up! Scamper back to Uglyville in the morning and find these cuddly critters:

Nothing says "high finance" like buttons, cookies, and...candy! Look around the bank for these sugary snacks:

The post office won't mail perishable food items, but if you want to come in *dressed* like a perishable food item, no problem. Can you find these fruity friends?

Still hungry? Head back to Babo's Cookies for a snack. While you're there, lend Babo a hand by finding these things he needs to make and bake his next batch:

Hey, over here! Search through the book and find me in every scene!